IS GOD A CUBS FAN?

By Arnold B. Kanter

Illustrated by Darlene Grossman

Cubs Season Summaries by Sam Eifling

JRC Press • Evanston, IL

Illustrations © 1999 by Darlene Grossman

First edition published by JRC Press, 303 Dodge Avenue, Evanston, IL 60202
847 328.7678
fax 847 328.2298

Published 1999
Printed in the United States of America.

ISBN: 0-9676415-0-0

The cost of printing this book was partially underwritten by an anonymous
donor in memory of her dear father, who was an avid Cubs fan and a *mensch*.

To everyone who has kept faith, hope, and
a sense of humor in the face of all odds.

CONTENTS

FOREWORD

When you write a book called *Is God a Cubs Fan?*, who do you ask to write the foreword?

Your rabbi, of course. (Presuming that is, that Ernie Banks is unavailable). So speaking in that capacity, dear reader, it gives me great pleasure to present this remarkable book to you. I say this because it is filled from cover to cover with wit, wisdom and heart—and you don't have to be Jewish *or* a baseball fan in order to enjoy it.

Is God a Cubs fan? Read on and I promise: you will eventually learn the answer to this important theological conundrum. Along the way you will learn a deeper truth as well: that baseball has a *neshamah*—that is to say, a uniquely Jewish soul.

But perhaps you are skeptical. If so, you should know that a growing number of experts are discovering a powerful symmetry between these two great spiritual traditions:

- Both baseball and Judaism are concerned with the mythic archetypes of exile and return. The ultimate goal of both traditions is homecoming. In baseball, players leave the safety of their dugout and run the base paths, with the hope of somehow finding the way to home plate. Likewise, since the destruction of the ancient Temple, the Jewish religion has been a veritable textbook for maneuvering through the perils of exile, guided by the dream of finally returning home.

- There are no fans anywhere who are as long-suffering as baseball fans. The plaintive cry coined by Brooklyn Dodger fans, "Wait till next year!" is most certainly a derivative of "Next year in Jerusalem!"—the refrain that ends every Passover Seder.

- Just as baseball is a uniquely Jewish sport, certain baseball teams are clearly more Jewish than others. The perennially tragic fates of teams such as the Boston Red Sox, the Brooklyn Dodgers and, of course, the Chicago Cubs have had an all-too-familiar resonance for Jewish baseball fans everywhere.

As I said earlier, however, you don't have to be Jewish to appreciate these truths. They are truly universal. Arnie Kanter's words will ring true for anyone who has ever poised on the edge of a dream, only to fall off.

Indeed, you will find that Arnie Kanter is the consummate tour guide for a journey into the glorious heartbreak that is Cubs baseball. Arnie is a native Chicagoan, and has suffered through countless losing seasons at Wrigley Field with a uniquely "Cubs-esque" combination of hope, fatalism, heartbreak and utter disgust. Most important, he has a pretty deep *neshamah* himself. And I should know. I'm his rabbi.

But enough about me. It's time to play ball!

—*Rabbi Brant Rosen*

INTRODUCTION

I was born a Cubs fan, and a Jew. Not necessarily in that
order. When the Cubs last played in the World Series, I was
two. I don't remember much about that, but I'm told they lost
to the Detroit Tigers in seven. That I can believe. My father, a
man several strides into his eighties now, was minus eight
years old when the Cubs last won the World Series. He tells
me that he doesn't remember much about it.

For better or worse—mainly worse—I remember a whole
lot about the Cubs, after the age of, say, five. Alas, the Cubs
occupied a large part of my life. As a child, I recall my sum-
mertime mood depending largely upon whether the Cubs
had won or lost that day. I had a pretty unhappy childhood.

I'm not going to try to relive all of the ups and downs—
and downs, and downs—of being a Cubs fan these past fifty
years. It's too painful. Most of those moments I regret I had
to live through once.

As most of us do, I've mellowed, perhaps even matured
a bit, as I've waxed senior. For some reason, though, that
process seems to have affected my relationship with the Cubs
little, if at all. In a world increasingly devoid of guideposts,

the Cubs have remained my North Star. Talk about lost. . . .

Increasingly, though, I've come to see connections between my North Star and my Jewish star. This connection is not something I set forth to find. It just happened. Slowly.

In 1983, I joined a Reconstructionist congregation. For those (many) who are not familiar with Reconstructionism, I'm sorry. But I certainly won't pretend to describe it in this book. For our purposes, it's probably sufficient to say that it is a branch of Judaism, dating back to 1922, that attempts to reconstruct the Jewish religion in a way that makes it speak more directly to modern Jews.

In Reconstructionism, tradition is important, but not controlling; it has a vote, but not a veto in matters of observance. Reconstructionists sometimes create their own traditions or rituals, often borrowing heavily from the past. Reconstructionism tends to be inclusive and non-judgmental. It rejects the notion that the Jewish people have been chosen by God. For me, Reconstructionism has provided meaning for many things that I used to do by rote.

The Jewish Reconstructionist Congregation (JRC), of Evanston, Illinois, of which I am a card-carrying member, has many traditions (we call them *minhagim*). One is an Open Mike during the afternoon of *Yom Kippur*. At the conclusion of the morning service on this holiest of Jewish holidays, members of the congregation are invited up to the *bimah* to speak for a couple minutes on anything of importance to them.

Most of these talks are serious reflections on important people, experiences, or causes in congregants' lives, listened to empathetically by the more than one hundred people who choose to remain at the *shul* (which, by the way, is a Methodist church rented by the congregation for the High Holidays, since the JRC synagogue building—purchased after years of heated congregational debate—was too small to house the congregation for High Holiday services from the moment it was purchased).

On *Yom Kippur,* 1984, without a great deal of planning or forethought, I found myself up on the *bimah,* reflecting on the existence of God, and discovering my answer in the Chicago Cubs. So enthusiastic was the reception to that talk, that I pursued it further the next *Yom Kippur*—and thus was a *minhag* born.

Each year I ponder the relationship between God and the Cubs, posing weighty questions that theologians have long wrestled with. For the past sixteen years, my talk has been the last one given at our Open Mike, placed there, I am told, because of the reluctance of others to follow what they may consider my off-the-wall remarks and because of a sense that anticipation of these remarks serves to hold the audience. I'm often asked for copies of these talks, and have been encouraged by congregants to publish them. This book is the fruit of that encouragement.

I'm not entirely new to this business. I've written five

satirical books on the law, a profession that I practiced for some fifteen years. These books were occasioned originally by a need to maintain my sanity in the face of seemingly insane, sometimes almost surrealistic, experiences that I encountered, first as an associate and then as a partner at a large and prestigious law firm, and, later, as a consultant to large law firms. Though I may not always have recognized it, these writings were born of love and of a need to understand. So, too, are the writings in this book.

I hope (and pray) that these pieces may rekindle in some readers moments in their lives when they have loved, or wondered, or just plain shaken their heads. And that, for others, this book may help them to understand those seemingly incomprehensible folk—whether they be fans of the Cubs or the Dodgers, of baseball or cricket, adherents of Judaism or Buddhism—whose passion for sport or religion, or both, may seem just a bit beyond the pale.

Each of the sixteen Open Mike talks is reprinted here pretty much as it was given, preceded by summaries of the sports year written—tongue planted firmly in cheek—by Sam Eifling, a student at Northwestern University's Medill School of Journalism, and accompanied by explanatory notes about the season or the congregation necessary for the general reader to appreciate what was said. The design of the book and the illustrations were done lovingly by JRC member, Darlene Grossman, and the entire project was shepherded through by the gentle staff of another JRC member, Dale Good.

In yore days, at the conclusion of the Passover *seder*, people said to one another, *"L'shana ha ba-a biyerushalayim,* next year may we meet in Jerusalem." To my friends, I wish, *"l'shana ha ba-a b'*Wrigley Field." And may the Cubs win the World Series again, come the millennium.

1984

Pennant Fever

By most Cubs' standards, 1984 was a downright magnificent year. They established a new home attendance record by drawing more than two million fans, they finished the season atop their division (with a 96–65 record), won the most games since capturing 98 in 1945, and were actually favored to go to the Fall Classic. To top it off, the team they edged by $6\frac{1}{2}$ games to win their division was the New York Mets, who beat out the Cubs for a playoff spot in the dregs of the 1969 season.

Individually, Rick Sutcliffe's 16–1 record earned him just the third Cy Young Award in the club's history. Second baseman Ryne Sandberg was the first Cub MVP since Mr. Cub himself, Ernie Banks, took two in a row in the late 50s. Skipper Jim Frey was named Manager of the Year. So why the long faces?

After winning their division, the Cubs whipped the San Diego Padres 13–0 and 4–2 in the first two games of the best-of-five National League Championship Series in Chicago, then proceeded to drop three straight on the West Coast. James Thompson, then Governor of Illinois, summed it up for many when he said "I feel like there's been a death in the family."

This was to be the fans' and players' absolution for a half century of going nowhere. "My ship has come in," said Ernie Banks before the National League Championship Series. "Good things come to those who wait . . . and wait . . . and wait."

So what do you say when you flip the wait light back on? "Nobody died here," Cubs outfielder Gary Matthews said. "We'll bounce back."

From success?

* *

Does God Exist?

'D LIKE TO TAKE A MINUTE to talk to you about God. Not in the manner of a born-again Christian because, personally, I think one birth's plenty. Do you remember how dark and wet it was in there, and then they give you this narrow little channel to scrunch yourself through? *Oy,* what a trauma birth was; I'm still recovering. But I digress.

As a youth, I first puzzled about God in Hebrew school at Rodfei Zedek, a conservative synagogue on the south side of Chicago, where other JRC luminaries such as Roger Price, Alan Gratch, and the Brothers Rubin (Neal and Alan), also puzzled. At least we puzzled on days that we weren't cutting Hebrew school to play baseball in East End Park, across the street from shul. In retrospect, I think that at Rodfei Zedek we learned God by rote. I don't mean to knock that. Rote works, at least on one level. Pleasant memories survive from those days, memories of beautiful melodies in a lovely sanctuary with a thought-provoking rabbi, memories of Sunday mornings when *bar-mitzvah*-age boys and their fathers ate bagels and lox and custard-filled pastries together, then bentched the blessings after the meal and ran across the street to play touch football.

After *Rodfei Zedek,* I next encountered God-puzzling in college, at Brandeis University. Now, though, our puzzling was no longer rote. We asked whether God existed. Could we prove it? Or was God, perhaps, dead. And when we studied the Book of Job, taught by a great scholar named Nahum Glatzer, we were left to wonder whether, if God indeed existed and was still alive, this was the sort of God we'd like to go out for a beer with, anyway (though I don't recall Professor Glatzer posing the question in quite that way).

After Brandeis, I took a break from my God-puzzling to attend law school and, then, to earn a few bucks as a lawyer. You might say that I drifted pretty far away from religion for the better part of twenty years, until, last year, we joined JRC. Here I found that not only was God not rote and God's existence questioned, but now I had to come to grips with the very real and troubling possibility that, if God existed, He might be a lady.

So, anyway, this High Holidays, I decided it's time—enough is enough. I'd devote the period between *Rosh Hashanah* and *Yom Kippur* to figuring out, once and for all, whether God existed. It wouldn't be easy, I knew, but what the hell.

Well, I've got some good news for you. God exists. And at the risk of seeming too much of a nutty, messianic-type personality, I would like to predict that God will soon make

His (or Her) presence visible to us in a manner such that none of us will ever again be able to doubt God's existence. As you break the fast tonight, watch for God' s presence . . . on television, manifesting Himself/Herself in the miracle of the Chicago Cubs reaching the World Series.

And one final thought, if we want to improve relations with our non-Jewish brothers and sisters, we need spread only one harmless little rumor—Ryne Sandberg[1] is Jewish.

---

[1] Cubs' star second baseman. (He is not Jewish.)

1985

Back to Reality

Baseball's universe righted itself quickly after the 1984 season: the Cubs began to lose again. It took a wave of injuries to drown the reigning division champs after they sailed along winning 34 of their first 53 games. The Cubs tied a club record by losing 13 straight games on the way to mediocrity, finally anchoring in fourth place in the division with just under a .500 winning percentage and sinking 23½ games behind the first-place St. Louis Cardinals.

Pitching did them in. Rick Sutcliffe finished 8–8 just a year after winning the Cy Young Award. Cub pitcher Reggie Patterson became the answer to a trivia question when Pete Rose notched his 4,191st hit off of Patterson, tying Ty Cobb's record. The one Cub pitcher, though, whose '85 record kept pace with his '84 performance was relief pitcher Lee Smith. His club-high 33 saves in '85 were all the more impressive considering how few saves were available. Of Lee Smith, Ray Sons wrote in the Chicago Sun Times, "Lee is saved for saves, and the Cubs are beyond saving."

There were the usual offensive bright spots for the Cubbies, provided by their only All-Star, Ryne Sandberg, who led the team with

26 home runs. (The Cubs did manage to lead the National League with 150 homers.) Ryno also stole 54 bases, the highest total by a Cub since "Wild Fire" Schulte swiped 57 bags in 1906.

But you can't keep Cubs' fans down—'84's coattails extended to push a club record 2.16 million fans through the turnstiles in '85.

From the Desk of God

SOME OF YOU MAY REMEMBER last *Yom Kippur,* when I predicted that God would manifest His or Her existence by ushering the Chicago Cubs into the World Series on *Yom Kippur* night. Well, the failure of that prediction to materialize generated quite a spiritual crisis within our congregation, and more than a little ugliness towards me, personally.

Leroy Shuster[1] took the Cubs' loss as proof that God was that within each of us that strove for what was good, and that there just wasn't enough striving within the Cubs. To Rabbi Arnie, of the White House,[2] it was proof that God worked in mysterious ways. And to Henry Waller,[3] with whom I went to Camp Indianola back in the 1950s, well poor Henry took it so hard that for a month he called me at 3:30 each morning and shouted, "Why did you do it?" But the most serious result of my faulty prediction was that

---

[1] One of the founders, and a former president, of JRC.

[2] JRC's rabbi, Arnie Rachlis, spent his sabbatical year serving as a White House Fellow in Washington, DC.

[3] JRC board member

I was sentenced to a year on the JRC Board of Directors.

So you'd think I'd have enough sense to keep my mouth shut this year, but noooo.

Actually, I have remained preoccupied with the existence of God. For *Chanukah* last year my daughters, Jodi and Wendy, bought me a pad of notepaper that says *From the Desk of God* at the top, with a thunderbolt through the *O*, and ever since, miraculously, my daughters have been receiving notes from God. They gave me permission to share the two most recent notes with you.

FROM THE DESK OF

September 24, 1985

Dear Jodes,

Many times I hear, "Why do the Jews fast on Yom Kippur?*" The short answer, of course, is "If not the Jews, who then?"*

Historically, non-Jews have rarely fasted on Yom Kippur, *unless they are unbelievably* frum. *While this could change any minute, I'm not counting on it. So it is left to the Jews to fast because I brought them out of Egypt, and for many other good reasons, as well.*

The first recorded fast was Harry Cohen, in 422, either B.C.E. or C.E., they forgot to record that; but, in any case, plenty long ago. Harry did not fast the entire day. He had a little nosh *around one and a banana at four thirty. Other than this, though, he abstained.*

The second recorded fast was in 1958—also, by coincidence, Harry Cohen (but a different one), who didn't eat all day, and died. This they don't print in the Bible.   —God

FROM THE DESK OF

September 24, 1985

Dear Wendzo,

Why do we blow the ram's horn to herald the New Year, and also for Yom Kippur? Though it's true that it is very difficult to blow the ram's horn and get that shrill sound, it is even more difficult to get that sound by blowing any other part of the ram; if you've ever tried, you know.

You may remember that as Abraham was about to sacrifice his son, Isaac, a ram appeared in the bush and Abraham burned the ram instead of Isaac. This may seem like a good thing to you, but the rams are not so nuts about the story. In fact, this explains why so few rams are Jewish (and also, perhaps, why so few Isaacs are rammish). Even the Los Angeles Rams football team has very few Jews on it, because most of them decided to become doctors or rabbis. Another reason is that the football is made of pig's skin, which is trayf, so many potential Hasidic superstars wouldn't touch it. Save the rams!   —God

For any of you who still doubt the existence of God, even after hearing these authentic letters—well, the Chicago Bears are 3 and 0.

1986

An UnBearable Year

The Cubs' downward spiral that had begun in 1985 continued to deepen into 1986. Jim Frey, who had been Manager of the Year just two years earlier, was fired in June as the Cubs wallowed near the bottom of their division. Gene Michaels was installed, but he could hardly stop the tailspin. Chicago finished 70–90, a full 37 games behind the first-place New York Mets. Said third-base coach Don Zimmer, "I don't think God could have come down and made this team win."

For the record, second-baseman Ryne Sandberg and catcher Jody Davis tried their best to compensate for God's (and the pitching staff's) shortcomings. Both were All-Stars and Gold Glove winners. Davis' 21 home runs paced the Cubs, who led the National League in homers for the second straight year with 155. Sandberg was again spectacular on defense, setting a major-league record by committing only five errors at second base and fielding a stellar .993 on the year.

But a rash of injuries to the pitching staff proved too much for the solid hitting and defense to overcome. Rick Sutcliffe's bum

shoulder led him into a dismal 5–14 showing, after going 24–9
over the two preceding years. Unfortunately, his misery invited
company as the Cubs' pitching staff lacked a 10-game winner
for the first time in their 111-year history and posted the highest
team ERA (4.49) in the National League. The axiom that
pitching is 50 percent of baseball proved true. The club settled
into a fifth-place finish in the NL Eastern Division with a
winning percentage of just .438.

●●●

The Refrigerator of Life

FOR TWO YEARS NOW, we have wrestled with the question
that our ancient rabbis and scholars have struggled with
over the centuries on *Yom Kippur.* Just what is
the relationship between God, the Jewish people, and sports,
anyway? Actually, I've been wrestling with that question. You
pretty much just sit there and listen (and I need hardly point
out that wrestling is itself a sport, but not one for a Jewish boy).

Now, of course, volumes have been written on the parallels
between the Cubs and the Jewish people. I mean, who can
attribute to mere coincidence the fact that the Jews wandered
for forty years in the desert and the Cubs have wandered for
more than forty years through the so-called "friendly confines"[1]
without winning a pennant—and without lights. And doesn't
Sandberg sound sorta Jewish to you? I know it does to me.

---

[1] Wrigley Field, home of the Cubs, is often referred to as the "Friendly
Confines," the description given to it by former Cub great, Ernie Banks.

But much less has been written on the parallels between the Chicago Bears and the Jewish people. Personally, I attribute this to the fact that, unlike the Jewish people, the Bears generally don't suffer much—their opponents do. This *Rosh Hashanah*, though, I began to ponder this question, prompted by something our rabbi said in his sermon. And for those of you who don't listen to our rabbi, maybe this will be a lesson to you as to what you can expect, if you do. Anyway, Arnie talked about how this Hebrew year, 5747, ends with the numbers 747 (not, in itself, a particularly astounding observation, I might add). For a horrible second I thought, oh, no, 747, he's going to call this the year of the jumbo jet and tell us more about his adventures in Washington. Instead, though, he pointed out how 7-4-7 add up to 18 (I confirmed this with my calculator) and how 18 stands for *chai* which means life.

Now what does all of this have to do with the Chicago Bears? Well, I suppose the answer is pretty obvious to most of you. Who is the Bears' popular folk hero this year? William "Refrigerator" Perry.[2] What is the Fridge's number? 72. And what is 72? Four *chai*. So I began combing the sporting goods stores all around Chicago to see whether anyone had recognized, and capitalized financially upon, this rather obvious fact. And, to my shock and dismay, I found that nobody had. So I had this sweatshirt made up. And since, besides listening to our rabbi, I also listened to our president talk on *Rosh Hashanah*

---

[2] A 300-pound-plus Bears lineman who, because of his tremendous bulk, was nicknamed "The Refrigerator."

about how the congregation needs funds, I'm going to suggest
to our fundraising committee that we have more of these
sweatshirts made up, and sell them for a mere four *chai* each.[3]

---

[3] Like most of my brilliant financial ideas, this one was never
implemented.

1987

Blank Check MVP

Since its opening in 1914, Wrigley Field has been known as a beautiful place to watch a baseball game—as they say, easy on the eyes. In 1987, it picked up an MVP-caliber player because it was easy on the knees, too.

After 11 years with the Montreal Expos, who play on artificial turf, outfielder Andre Dawson decided his knees needed soft grass underneath them, and practically got down on one of them asking the Cubs to sign him. Pitcher Rick Sutcliffe was so excited about the prospect of playing with Dawson that he said he'd donate $100,000 toward signing him. After numerous snubs and snags from the Cubs' front office, Dawson presented the Cubs with a signed contract with the salary amount left blank. The Cubs filled in a bargain-basement price of $500,000. Dawson was worth every cent.

Andre won a Gold Glove award, as did second baseman Ryne Sandberg, but Dawson's true calling was as a slugger. He slammed 49 home runs, the most by a Cub since Hack Wilson in 1930. He batted .296 with 137 RBIs, became only the 12th Cub to hit for the *cycle[1] on April 29 and established a modern Cubs record for home runs in a month with 15 in August. (August was also the month that the Cubs retired Hall-of-Famer Billy Williams' number 26, which now flies at Wrigley Field from the flag pole in right, where he played outfield.) Andre led the National League in home runs, RBIs and total bases. Fans in the right field bleachers began to greet their star, as he trotted out to his position, with a stand-and-bow routine known as "salaams."*

For his remarkable year, Dawson won the MVP award—the first time the award had gone to a player on a last-place team. Rick Sutcliffe also had a banner year, winning 18 games and falling just two votes shy of the Cy Young award. Still, the team found winning difficult, finishing 76–85. After a brief fling in first place in late May, the Cubs generously let every other team in the NL East pass, handing out a team-record 628 walks along the way.

Cubs fans apparently didn't mind much, though: The '87 team became the first last-place NL team to draw over 2 million in home attendance.

The Sacrificing by Isaac

FOR THE LAST THREE *Yom Kippurs* (or is it *Yoms Kippur?*), I have spoken about God and Judaism and sports. And a lot of you have laughed. And I have to tell you now that that laughter has hurt me deeply. Because those talks were not meant to be funny. I take my God seriously and I take my

---

[1] Hit a single, double, triple and home run in one game.

Judaism seriously and, most of all, I take my sports seriously. So, this year, I decided not to risk being misunderstood and, in lieu of speaking of the Cubs or the Bears (about both of which there is precious little to say, in any case), I decided to talk about the *Rosh Hashanah Torah* portion in which God instructs Abraham to take his favorite son, Isaac, up to Mount Moriah and there to bind him and offer him as a sacrifice.

Now, of course, scholars have struggled with this *parsha* for centuries. What kind of a God would ask Abraham to give up his most loved son? What kind of a man would offer up his son, even at the insistence of God? And I read many interpretations of the story, some claiming that God was merely testing Abraham, some arguing that it was Abraham testing God. And all of these interpretations are interesting, but none of them seems to me satisfactory.

So I began my own search for an explanation that would be true to the text and might, at the same time, allow me to emerge with my respect for both God and Abraham intact. This search has not been easy. It has led me back to inspect many original historical documents—the Dead Sea Scrolls, the Red Sea Scrolls, several boxes of letters in Abraham's own hand. And, at last, I believe I have found the answer.

Abraham was very old—100 years when Isaac was born. And we know Abraham was hard of hearing. This we can discern directly from the *Torah*. How? When God speaks to Abraham and tells him to take Isaac to Mount Moriah, he says, " Take your son," and, though the text does not reflect it, Abraham says, "Huh?" And, so, God continues, "your

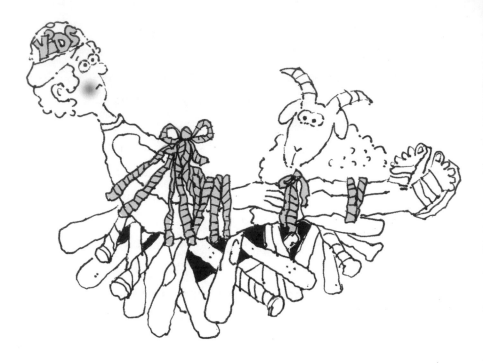

favored one" and Abraham says, "Eh?" and God finally shouts, "*ISAAC!*" Later, when Abraham is about to kill Isaac, you will recall that the angel has to shout to him twice, "Abraham, Abraham," because Abraham does not hear the angel the first time.

Now we know that Isaac was not a young child when he was taken by Abraham to Moriah. And from the Red Sea Scrolls, I discovered—and this is not generally known—that Isaac was quite athletic. Indeed, he played left field for the Yisraeli *Yids.* And, just before God spoke to Abraham, it is recorded in those scrolls, the *Yids* had dropped a real heart-breaker to the Philistine Pirates, 5–4, when Isaac grounded into a game-ending triple play, with men on first and second and nobody out. This loss dropped the *Yids* into a tie for second place.

Now the Lord was plenty ticked off at Abraham, Isaac's coach, when this happened, and He spoke to Abraham saying, not, as the Bible says, "Take your son, your favored one, Isaac, whom you love, and go to the land of Moriah, and offer him there as a sacrifice on one of the heights which I will point out to you," but rather, "When you take your son, your favored son, Isaac, whom you love and go to the field of the first place Moriah Mountaineers, tell him there to sacrifice, when I point it out to you." So, in the *Akedah*, God is not testing Abraham at all, but reprimanding him for his lousy baseball strategy. And the real pathos in the story is that old Abraham's defective hearing almost turned a sacrifice bunt into a sacrifice of his son, thus converting the bunting of Isaac into the binding of Isaac. Out of this near tragic episode, the rabbis tell us, came the use of hand signals to batters.

1988

All-Stars in the Dark

Sandwiched between Andre Dawson's incredible 1987 season and the miraculous 1989 season was a pedestrian fourth-place Cubs finish in 1988. The most historically significant of the 77 wins that year came on August 9, when the Cubs beat the New York Mets 6–4. Defeating the Mets is always cause for celebration, but this particular victory came in the first night game ever played at Wrigley Field. For the first time in the 74-year history of Wrigley, no one had to skip school or work to go root for the Cubs on a Monday.

A more dubious Wrigley tradition persisted, however—the Cubs produced some outstanding individual performances en route to losing more than half their games. Pitcher Greg Maddux blossomed early in the season and finished 18–8. At 22, the right-hander became the youngest ever Cub All-Star, and the first Cub since 1971 to defeat every team in the league at least once. No other Cub starter finished above .500 for the year, though Rick Sutcliffe did manage to steal home on July 29.

Coming off his MVP year, Andre Dawson again led the team in home runs (24) and RBIs (79). He hit .303, earned his 8th Gold

Glove award, and set a major league record with his twelfth straight season with at least 10 home runs and 10 stolen bases. Ryne Sandberg added to his growing legend by whapping his 100th career home run. First baseman Mark Grace was named Sporting News NL Rookie of the Year after hitting .296—the best for a Cubs rookie in 15 years. Oddly enough, all seven of his home runs that year were on the road.

But even with six All-Stars on the roster, the Cubs finished a dismal 24 games back of the first-place Dodgers. Manager Don Zimmer didn't see much reason to expect better than a .500 finish in 1989. Zim was known for his keen baseball instincts, but as it turned out, he dropped the ball on that prognostication.

● ●

Does God Want Lights in Wrigley Field?

L ET ME BE HONEST. I was going to skip the Open Mike this year. But the demand was so overwhelming—not one, but two people asked me whether I was going to speak— that, in the end, I've relented.

In past years, I've touched not only on God, but sports. This year, the natural choice would have been to turn to the Olympics. But when I heard the groans that greeted Rabbi Arnie on *erev Rosh Hashanah* when he referred to the High holidays as our s-o-u-l Olympics,[1] I quickly canned that idea. Thanks a lot, Rabbi.

By the way, I almost missed *erev Rosh Hashanah* altogether,

---

[1] The 1988 Olympics were held in Seoul, South Korea.

because of the finals of the U.S. Open tennis tournament. For those of you of Orthodox background, who felt compelled to leave early to get to services on time, Mats Willanderstein beat Ivan Lendlberg in five sets.[2] Tennis, of course, is a great Jewish game. Though it is not generally known, tennis was invented by a group of rabbis. How do I know this? Easy. You think maybe a bunch of *goyim* would have come up with a scoring system that goes—love, fifteen, thirty and forty, with six games to a set, and foot faults?

But enough frivolity. I want to try to put to rest, once and for all, the question that Chicago rabbis have struggled with all year—does God want lights in Wrigley Field? In seeking to answer this question, I turned first to the text of the *Torah*. There, I was surprised to find remarkably little on point. I know that some would point to the opening verses of Genesis, in which, as many of you may recall, God created light and saw that it was good. But, according to Rashi,[3] this passage refers to daylight, not to ballpark lights. Rashi concluded, therefore, that God did not want night games.

Moses Maimonides[4] (whose views, in my opinion, are afforded far too much weight just because of his first name) came to exactly the opposite view. Oddly enough, the views of another Moses, Moses Malone[5], are afforded only about

---

[2] Mats Willander beat Ivan Lendl in a match that ended just as services were scheduled to begin.

[3] Great commentator on the *Torah,* not to be confused with Vic Rashi, pitcher for the New York Yankees in the 1950s.

[4] Another famous scholar and commentator.

[5] A very large professional basketball player.

average weight, unless he looks like he might be inclined to fight about them, in which case they are afforded a healthy deference. (Malone, however, is paid a lot more than Maimonides ever was. Maimonides was an excellent point guard, but suffered greatly in his compensation because all of his team's games happened to be on Friday night and Saturday, and he was *shomer shabbos*.) So far as I know, Moses Malone has never expressed an opinion as to whether God wanted lights in Wrigley Field.

Speaking of Moses, most of you recall when the Red Sea parted. I don't mean that you actually recall it, but you've probably read about it. Often, when I read the *Torah*, I long for the good old days of miracles and signs from the Lord—rods turning into serpents, frogs, locusts—those sorts of things. And every once in awhile, those signs still appear. In this driest and hottest of all summers, where drought struck the entire country, can anyone really believe that it was a coincidence that the Cubs first scheduled night game was rained out?

Sometimes God's meanings aren't all that mysterious.

1989

Pennant Fever Again

The forecast for 1989 called for another drought when the Cubs went an ignominious 9–23 in spring exhibition games. But when they started playing for keeps, the outlook changed. The Cubs held first place for 25 straight days in May and June, and were only a game and a half behind the Montreal Expos at the All-Star break.

Credit the mercurial performances of first-years Dwight Smith, Lloyd McClendon and Jerome Walton for the Cubs' sudden fortunes. Credit Manager Don Zimmer's brash, savvy play calling that earned him Manager of the Year honors. Credit improved pitching from Greg Maddux and Rick Sutcliffe. Credit 36 saves by acquisition Mitch "Wild Thing" Williams. Credit the Cubbies. They skipped their traditional early September swoon and clinched the division by the 26th, finishing 93–69, six games in front of the New York Mets.

For the first time ever, the Cubs finished with the highest batting average in the National League two years in a row. Ryne Sandberg hit 30 home runs, the most by a Cubs second baseman in 70 years and set a record by playing 90 consecutive errorless games after June 20. Jerome Walton won the National League Rookie of the Year award, the first Cub since 1962 to do so. If that weren't proof enough of the Cubs young talent, Dwight Smith finished second in the voting.

The Cubs faced the San Francisco Giants in the Championship Series. In 1908, your ancestors might recall, the Cubs beat the Giants, who at that time hailed from Brooklyn, on the Cubs' way to their last World Series title of the century. Would the Cubs atone for their 1984 meltdown against the Padres?

Sophomore first baseman Mark Grace did his best to pull the Cubs into the Fall Classic with his 11 hits for 17 at bats, 8-RBI performance in the five game series. However, his Giant counter-part, Will Clark, set major league records with 13 hits, 8 runs, and a mammoth .650 batting average in leading the Giants to a 4–1 series win. The sun sets in the West, after all, and the Cubs' sur-prising flood of success finally evaporated.

The team that spent so much of the season in first place also had, as usual, first-rate fans. Almost 2.5 million of them swept through Wrigley Field turnstiles, the most in 114 years of Cubs baseball. When the Cubs rein, fans pour in.

An earthquake struck San Francisco during the World Series, postponing several games. Alas, no quake struck Chicago.

* *

Is Baseball Anti-Semitic?

'M NOT HAPPY TO BE HERE. For me, Open Mike evokes some of the worst moments of my life.

In 1984, my first Open Mike, I predicted that God would prove His existence as He sent the Cubs into the

World Series by beating the San Diego Padres. You all know what happened. And many members of this congregation have not forgotten yet. Each year, when I hear the rabbi say how everyone should forgive everyone else for the sins they may have inadvertently committed, I think, "Aha, this year they're going to flock up to me and say, 'Arnie, we forgive you, we know you didn't do that on purpose.'" But has even one person come up to say that to me—*hell no*.

Some of you may have expected me to moan and groan about the Cubs being down three games to one in the play-offs, just taking the field for the fifth game as we sit here. But that doesn't bother me. It's just not their turn yet. Geez, they won it all in 1908, do you expect them to do it *every* year?

No, what bothers me is that this year I have been forced to confront, head-on, a very painful fact, the fact that the sport I love most, baseball, is anti-Semitic. To be honest, I've suspected it for some time. But, until this year, I've swept it under the rug.

Why did I suspect it? Little things. They add a team in San Diego and what do they call them—the San Diego *Padres*. And the St Louis Cardinals? Sure, they have a *bird* on the uniform, but they don't fool this Jew. Have you heard of the New York Rabbis or the Philadelphia *Chazans*? No, neither have I. And you go out to the game and try to get something to eat. Do they serve *knishes*? *Gefilte* fish? No, hot dogs, *trayf*.

So I suspected it. But, this year, they prove it. What do they do? Schedule Cubs playoff games on both *erev Yom Kippur* and *Yom Kippur* afternoon. When I pointed out this clear anti-Semitism to a friend, he said I was overreacting.

"First of all," he said, "the Cubs don't have any Jewish players, so it won't affect them."

"Well, that's what a lot of people think," I said. "But it's not true, they do have a Jewish player, a starter, he just changed his name so that people don't know it."

Well, my friend perked up at this. "Who is it?" he asked.

"Promise not to tell anyone," I said, "because this guy really doesn't want it to be known."

"I promise," my friend said.

"Okay, *Shayna* Dunstein,[1] the shortstop."

"Noooo," my friend said in disbelief. "But even so, that doesn't prove anti-Semitism, he protested. Not only Jews are Cubs fans," he said.

Well, I've decided to test that out. How many of you here today are Cubs fans, raise your hand. Okay, now how many of you are Jewish?

Uh-huh, just what I thought.

Anyway, all of this raises the ethical question, can we watch the Cubs on *Yom Kippur?* Frankly, I was shocked and dismayed that there are not television monitors positioned around the sanctuary during the service. Seriously. I figure that if we can have a video camera on *Rosh Hashanah* to attract a couple of Lutheran German clergy, we sure as hell can have some TVs on *Yom Kippur* to attract several hundred Chicago-area Jews.[2]

---

[1] Really, Shawon Dunston

[2] In a controversial decision, the rabbi allowed a local TV station to film the Lutheran bishop of Berlin and his entourage, who came as guests of the congregation during *Rosh Hashanah* services.

But, we've got to face reality. Look around. There are no TVs.

So, what to do—go home to watch the game or stay at services? Well, I think that this one is really between each person and his or her God. But, I can tell you what I'm going to do after Open Mike—go to a study group here, and I'll tell you why. I like to avoid ethical questions whenever possible, and this one's easy. One of two things is going to happen this afternoon. Either the Cubs will win, and then I'll be able to see them play game six on Wednesday. Or they lose—and, I ask you, do I need the aggravation of watching them do that, on an empty stomach, yet?

So, today I'll be *frum*. Now if this were the seventh game, *oy*, would I have something to repent for next year.

1990

Going Fourth Once More

In 1985, coming off a division title, the Cubs finished 77–84, in fourth place. In 1990, again coming off a division title, the Cubs finished 77–85, in fourth place.

The Cubs had history on their side. In 1945, the year they last went to a World Series, the Cubs finished in first place, 89-63. Two years after that, the Cubs were 69–85, in sixth place. Of course, it used to be harder to manage 85 losses, back when the seasons were 154 games. But the Cubs were equal to the task.

Even the burden of history couldn't account for the team's 1990 plummet, though; the cast was almost identical to 1989's, indicating that the previous year, as many had suspected, was a fluke. You can hardly blame skipper Don Zimmer for trying to lighten the clubhouse mood occasionally. The grizzled old cherub was capable of almost anything, both on and off the field.

On July 18, when Greg Maddux hadn't won in 13 starts, Zimmer announced that he'd swim Lake Michigan if his star right-hander beat the Padres that day. Maddux went out and won 4–2. After being inundated with flippers and goggles, Zimmer, laughingly, admitted that he didn't even know how to swim.

In the final game of the season, the Cubs faced the Philadelphia Phillies with only fourth place at stake. Hearing that outfielder Andre Dawson had joked that he was going to manage that night's game, Zimmer said, "Tell him he can manage." Dawson, who led the club with a .310 average and 104 RBIs that year, finished the season 1–0 as a manager. Maddux threw eight innings and batted in a crucial run when Dawson gave him the hit sign on a 2–0 count in the fifth.

Sure, Dawson could manage. The question has always been, can the Cubs?

• •

Reconstructing the Season

T'S GOOD TO BE BACK UP at the pulpit at our little *shul*-away-from-*shul*.[1] I was happy to hear Arnie say on *Rosh Hashanah* that the pastor of this *shul* is going to visit our *shul*. I'm planning to come when he does. Not because I'm that interested in what he has to say. But I can't wait to see whether they cover up our ark and *shlep* over a cross.[2]

But I digress. Once again, I find myself under enormous pressure. You may think this melodramatic or lacking in humility, but, from talking to you all on *Rosh Hashanah*, it seems to me that about 70 percent of the attendance on *Yom Kippur* is attributable to baseball *midrashim* rather than atonement. Now, I would never actually say that, because I know it would hurt

---

[1] In 1989, services were held at a local school. In 1990, they returned to our regular spot—First United Methodist Church.

[2] Each year the congregation moves a portable ark that holds the *Torah* over to the church, and we cover up the prominent carvings of Jesus and saints behind the altar.

Rabbi Arnie deeply—and then I'd know that I was one of those people he forgives from the pulpit each year.[3] But if, perchance, he overhears this, I want to ask his forgiveness, even if what I say is perfectly true—which we all know it is.

But what to talk about? The perennial problem. I suppose I could turn to optimistic topics, like the Bears being 3–0. Or the Bulls' prospects for this year. Or I could wax nostalgic, about the White Sox' last year of playing in Comiskey Park, and all the happy memories from there. But, let's be honest, how many of you are breaking the fast at Comiskey Park for the last night game there?

But *Yom Kippur* is not a time for optimism and nostalgia. No. It's a time for wallowing in misery. So I must revert to the primary source of real misery for all Jews—the Chicago Cubs. Oh, I know there are problems in the world that some might consider more serious—anti-Semitism, Saddam Hussein, homelessness. Yes, those are serious, too. But, somehow, the Cubs' predicament seems quintessentially Jewish. Particularly so because I've always had the nagging feeling that we Jews should be able to do something to solve it. Until recently, though, the answer had eluded me. This year, I figured it out. What the Cubs need is a Reconstructionist approach to baseball.

Look, follow me, here's what we do. First, we get Arnie selected commissioner of baseball. Hell, if he can be elected

---

[3] Rabbi Arnie Rachlis used to publicly ask forgiveness from the *bimah* from anyone he might have offended in the prior year.

president of the Chicago Board of Rabbis,[4] getting him named commissioner ought to be a piece of *challah*. If necessary, we organize. We ask, "just how long has it been since we've had a Jewish commissioner?" We strike—we refuse to eat hot dogs (do you really believe the kosher hot dogs at the ballpark are kosher?). If necessary, we stay away from games altogether.

So they elect Arnie. "What then?" you ask. I'll tell you what then, if you'll just be a little patient. Baseball ends around *Yom Kippur*, right? And the Cubs are rarely in first place then. But, as Reconstructionist Jews, who decides when *Yom Kippur* comes—damn right, Rabbi Arnie. I'll be looking for *Yom Kippur* around May 15 next year, when the Cubs are in first. Then we do the same thing with the playoffs and the World Series, they end when Rabbi Arnie says they end—and if that just happens to be when the Cubs are leading, well so be it.

"But is this fair?" you ask. "Does it give each team an equal chance?" Don't talk to me about equality, talk to me about justice. How many of you can still see the ground ball going through Leon Durham's legs in 1984? Every night I see it.

There are other benefits to this approach. Think of what it will do for the Reconstructionist movement in general, and for membership in JRC. Of course, this growth will create some problems. We will no longer be able to hold High Holiday Services in this church/shul—it will be much too small. Fortunately, with Arnie as commissioner, the solution is clear—*l'shana ha ba-a b'*Wrigley Field.

---

[4] Incredibly, Arnie, as a Reconstructionist, was elected president of the Board, which is dominated by more traditional rabbis.

1991

Paying for Mediocrity

Baseball teams can be like gifts to your mom: Spending more doesn't necessarily make them better. A case in point would be the 1991 Cubs, who increased their payroll by more than 90 percent over the 1990 club, but won the same number of games, 77, and again finished fourth.

The Cubs were mathematically eliminated from playoff contention on September 18. They beat the New York Mets that day, but the Pittsburgh Pirates also won, solidifying their claim to the division crown. The Chicago Tribune *headline the next morning summed it up well: "Maddux shines, but Cubs still eliminated." Greg Maddux picked up his 12th victory (to go with 10 losses), but was understandably subdued afterwards. "I felt like I've let some games slip away this year," he said. "That's behind me now. I remember those games, but I don't worry about them. There's nothing I can do about it now."*

Maddux need not have hung his head, though. He was the only pitcher to throw even one shutout for the Cubs (he threw two) and led the staff in wins (15), starts (37), innings pitched (263), strike-

outs (198) and offensive runs scored (8). The only other starter with as many as 10 wins was Mike Bielecki, who finished 13–11 with an ERA of 4.50. Southpaw reliever Chuck McElroy set a club rookie record for appearances (71) on his way to six wins, three saves and a 1.95 ERA.

But if you're the finger-pointing type, you must look at the batting lineup first. The only Cub to hit above .300 for the year was substitute Doug Strange, who in three games went 4-for-9 at the plate. Among regulars, Ryne Sandberg's .291 led a team that hit an aggregate .253. Andre Dawson's 31 home runs accounted for about a fifth of the team's league-leading total of 159, but he hit for only a .272 average.

Manager Don Zimmer was canned on May 20. Joe Altobelli managed the 38th game of the season, an 8–6 loss to the Mets, and was subsequently succeeded by Jim Essian, who was fired on October 19.

Meanwhile, in another part of the city, the Chicago Bulls won their first NBA championship. The franchise had been around since the 1966/67 season, so it took them a while. But Chicago sport fans know about patience.

Converting the Heathen

ET ME BE HONEST—it's nice to be the only Arnie up on the bimah.[1]

I don't want to give you the wrong impression. Arnie has had a very profound influence on my life. Many of you

---

[1] Rabbi Arnie Rachlis was on sabbatical.

may be unaware that, when I joined this congregation, my name was Chayim Kanter.

It's not just Arnie's name that's influenced me, though, but his actions as well. Right now, for example, Arnie's in Southern California, spreading the gospel-according-to-Kaplan,[2] trying to tilt wayward Jews towards Reconstructionism. I may be way off here, but I envision him leading a sort of modern-day crusade of Volvos and BMWs down the freeways of Los Angeles, seeking to convert the heathen.

Don't get me wrong, I think that's very important work. Like the rest of you, I've been shocked and dismayed to read the articles about how many Jews we're losing, through intermarriage and otherwise. Personally, though, I think we should be taking a far more aggressive approach to this problem than Arnie is. It's fine to try to bring drifting Jews home to Judaism, but why not go after that huge market of people who have never experienced the joys of *Yiddish*? That's where the real opportunity lies.

So I asked myself, what's keeping more people from converting to Judaism? I pondered this during last Saturday night's Cubs-Expos game (which, with an incredible comeback from a 5–0 deficit, the Cubs won 7–5 in ten innings). Of course, as a sensitive human being, I felt great joy after that game. But I wondered why I did not feel fulfillment as a Jew, why I didn't feel *nachas*. The answer became clear to me on the El trip home: the entire experience was *goyish*. Indeed,

---

[2] Mordecai Kaplan, the founder of Reconstructionism.

glancing down at my scorecard, I noticed that not a single Cubs player is Jewish. Now that fact might not cause those of us who have endured the pain of circumcision and the trauma of *bar mitzvah* to leave the faith. But who the hell would want to convert to a religion that not a single Cub player would choose? Not me, that's for sure. So I've hatched a plan to make attending Wrigley Field a more Jewish experience next season. Here are the steps I've taken so far:

1. The team name has been changed to the Chicago *Cubbelas.*

2. Next year, when a home run is hit, you'll hear Harry Caray shout, "There's a long drive, it might be, it could be, it is a home run, *VAY IZ MIR!*"[3]

3. During the first rain delay next year, Steve Stone is going to reveal that Andre Dawson has agreed to change his name back to his original—*Avram Dawstein.*

4. Vendors will sell gefilte fish with little packets of red and white horseradish; and *Mogen David* wine instead of *Budweiser*—but not after the seventh inning.

5. Before turning the lights on for night games Wayne Messmer will recite a *bracha* ending with *"l'hadlik ner shel Cubbelas."*[4]

6. The name "Bleacher Bums" has been changed to "Bleacher *Bochers.*"

---

[3] Caray used to end his home run calls with "HO–LY COW!"

[4] Messmer sings the "Star Spangled Banner" at Cubs home games. The suggestion is that he switch to a blessing over the lights.

7. On June 16, the first 5,000 fans to enter the park will receive *mezzuzot*.

8. After each *Cubbela* victory, the fans will put their arms around each other and chant *shehehianu*.[5]

9. And, finally, we have bought advertising time and I'm proud to announce that Reconstructionism has been named the official religion of the Chicago *Cubbelas*.

This plan is not going to be cheap. But the future of American Jewry may well hinge on its success. So I appeal to you all to contribute as generously as you can to the new American Jewry/Chicago *Cubbela* fund that's been established at JRC. Next year, we'll not just get excited about a *Cubbela* victory—we'll *kvell*. *L'shana haba-a b'*Wrigley Field.

---

[5] A traditional prayer of thanks, sung in JRC with people putting their arms around one another.

1992

Say Goodbye to Cy

*Despite the amazing year pitcher Greg Maddux had in 1992—
National League Cy Young Award, Gold Glove Award, All-Star
starter, 20–11 record, tied for the league lead in victories, third-
lowest ERA (2.18)—he will be remembered best by Cubs fans for
what he didn't do: re-sign with the Cubs.*

*After the best year by a Cubs pitcher since Rick Sutcliffe in
1984, Maddux went to the Atlanta Braves as a free agent, signing
for $28 million over five years, just $500,000 more than the Cubs
had offered. In Atlanta, he won the next three Cy Young Awards.
New Cubs general manager Larry Hines had been lax in renewing
Maddux's contract, and Maddux, probably the pitcher of the decade
for the 1990s, had other options.*

*Maddux went on to win a World Series with the Braves while
the Cubs . . . well, the Cubs were consistently the Cubs. They
finished in fourth place in 1992 for the third straight year, and
at 78–84, had just one more win than they'd had in either of the
previous two years. In the eight years since going to the National
League Championship Series in 1984, the club had won 76, 77, or
78 games six times.*

It wasn't as though the club didn't play well—it was more that
they didn't play well until they had settled at the bottom of the
division. The Cubs hadn't won 18 games in a month since July
1989, but they won 18 in both June and August. They set defen-
sive marks for most errorless games in a season (88) and highest
fielding percentage (.982). And Hines finagled a trade that sent
unhappy slugger George Bell to the White Sox in exchange for
future MVP Sammy Sosa.

The other Cubs All-Star besides Maddux was stalwart Ryne
Sandberg, who made his ninth appearance at the midsummer classic.
He led NL second basemen in assists (539) for the seventh time and
didn't commit a throwing error for the second consecutive season.
He also hit 26 home runs and batted .304. Appropriately, Sandberg
became the game's highest-paid player when the Cubs awarded him
a four-year, $30.5 million extension in spring training.

Were it not for a baldheaded icon playing basketball on the South
Side, Sandberg might have been Chicago's most beloved athlete.
But since the Michael Jordan–led Chicago Bulls won their second-
straight NBA title, Sandberg couldn't even claim to be the city's
favorite number 23.

Sin in the Bleachers

O)Y, WHAT TO TALK ABOUT this year?
I've had a lot of suggestions. Many people have
come up and asked why I always have to talk about
the Cubs. *Yom Kippur* is depressing enough. Why not talk
about the Bulls this year, they ask. And I must admit, that is

tempting. After all, the Bulls are a Chicago team. And they have won two world championships in a row. So why not talk about the Bulls?

I'll tell you why not. I ask you, is professional basketball a Jewish sport? Can a Jewish guy really relate to ten Goliaths racing up and down the court at about a zillion miles an hour when his people took forty years to cross a damn desert? That's right, forty years. And you know how far they actually went, I mean if they'd gone in a straight line—less than 250 miles. That's 6 miles a year, or 29 yards a day, or, if you figure an eight hour work day, less than 4 yards an hour. At that rate, it would take 3½ days to get from here to the Davis Street Fishmarket.[1] If this is the pace at which your ancestors traveled, are you going to enjoy professional basketball? I don't think so.

Another thing about basketball, it's anti-Semitic. Did you ever notice all those guys who, before they shoot a free throw, cross themselves? But did you ever see anybody *davenning* at the free throw line? I mean they've got enough for a *minyan*, there are ten of them out there. But do they *daven*? No.

And another thing, they call it the free throw line, or the charity line, but do you ever hear them call it the *tzedakah* line? Hell, no.

And do you see any Jewish guys on the Bulls? No. And you're not likely to, either. Just try to imagine the Bulls

---

[1] A restaurant located a block from the church where JRC High Holiday services are held.

announcer at the stadium—the lights go out and spotlights swirl all around as he calls out, "and in the middle, wearing number eighteen, *chai,* from Yeshiva University, Kareem-Abdul Goldstein."

No, basketball is not a game you talk about on *Yom Kippur.* Baseball is a game you talk about on *Yom Kippur.* But what to say? For the last two and a half weeks I have been in something of a dither. Just seventeen days ago today the Cubs were mathematically eliminated from this year's division race. Of course a big surprise to me is something this did not come as. Then why should it bother me? (Not that it bothers me that much. I mean I'm functioning—sort of. Well it has been only seventeen days. It's not like I've had months to get over this.)

I have to be honest, though. At times I have despaired. Just the other day, in a weak moment, I said to my wife, "Why couldn't I have been born in Oakland?" But it is not the tradition of Jews to despair. (Okay, it is, but we're trying to break out of it.) In my more religious moods I feel confident that all of this is part of a plan that God has for Cubs fans. Not a very good plan, perhaps, but a plan. So the question becomes, just what is God's plan for the Cubs? Why, with the talent they've had for the last three years, have they not won a pennant? Have we Cubs fans committed some grievous sin that has prevented that? Unfortunately, I'm afraid the answer to that question is *yes.*

I came to this conclusion three days ago as Carol and I sat out at the last Cubs game of the season and watched Andre

Dawson belt his 399th career home run to give the Cubs a 3–2 victory. *Oy*, did we *kvell*. But what happened immediately after Dawson's home run? He jogs back out to right field— and the people in the bleachers bow down to him. Now what is the first commandment that Moses lugged all the way down with him from the top of Sinai? "I am the Lord your God, you shall have no other gods beside Me."

Is it any wonder, then, that the Cubs have not won a pennant, when their fans blatantly flaunt the first commandment? But what are we to do? Can we convince the fans in the right field bleachers that bowing down to Dawson is costing the Cubs a pennant? Not bloody likely. No, I have concluded, reluctantly, that for the Cubs to win a pennant they must let Andre Dawson go.

But I have some very bad news for us, even if the Cubs do trade Dawson. The second commandment says, "For I the Lord your God am an impassioned God, visiting the guilt of the fathers upon the children, upon the third and upon the fourth generations." So it looks to me like it'll be late 21st century— at the earliest—before we Cubs fans can hope for a pennant.

And they wonder why we Jews despair.

1993

Finishing Strong

Now, looking back, it seems like quite a feat that the 1993 squad managed the third winning season for the Cubs in twenty years. The front office allowed free agents Greg Maddux and Andre Dawson to slip away to the Atlanta Braves and the Boston Red Sox, respectively. Maddux had led the team in wins for five straight years; Dawson had led the team in RBIs for three—no major league team had ever before lost that combination of productivity. Maddux's alleged replacement, free agent Jose Guzman, formerly of the Texas Rangers, went just 12–10 on a tendinitis-afflicted shoulder; Maddux meanwhile went 20–10 for Atlanta. The Cubs were sucker-punched when Dawson's replacement, Candy Maldonado, another costly free agent, batted .186 before he was traded to the Cleveland Indians on August 8.

Given all that, an 84–78 record doesn't seem too bad. Heading into the final month of the season, the Cubs were six games below .500 and only 7½ above the expansion Florida Marlins. They then reeled off 20 wins in their next 28 games, due largely to the steady pitching of Greg Hibbard (15–11) and Jose Bautista (10–3), who

combined for a 10–1 record in September. Free-agent acquisition
Randy Meyers also chipped in 15 saves that month. He struck out
86 in just over 75 innings' work, and set a National League record
with 53 saves for the year.

Meyers made the accusation in September that some of his team-
mates weren't "winners," adding that "all they care about is their
stats." He probably noticed burgeoning star Sammy Sosa's 33 home
runs and 36 stolen bases, 20 of which came in a frantic last two
months of the season. His 30/30 year was the first in Cubs history.
But even with such gaudy numbers, Sosa batted a mediocre .261.
He was widely thought to be too impatient and self-absorbed to meld
his glamour stats into an all-around team contribution. Just wait.

● ●

Finding the Messiah

S OME OF YOU MAY HAVE NOTICED that we have a new rabbi
this year.[1] Well I noticed that, too, and it seemed to me
that he might like it if his congregants did not waste
time on *Yom Kippur* talking about the Cubs. So I decided to
talk about something serious, but not somber—not sports—
at Open Mike this year. . . .

But then I got to thinking about it. I've been doing this for
ten years now. It's become a tradition. And along comes a
new rabbi and all of a sudden I shouldn't say what I want to
say at Open Mike? Because we hired some big-shot clergy-

---

[1] After a two-year search for a rabbi, the congregation hired Richard
Hirsh. The comments about him in this talk are entirely untrue.

man from the East, I should give up my First Amendment rights? Because he went to the Reconstructionist Rabbinical College in Philadelphia, and probably he's a Phillies fan, I should not mention the Cubs because it might—heaven forbid—offend our new rabbi? Y'know we weren't doing so badly around JRC without a rabbi for two years.

I'm not knocking the rabbi. His sermon about brokenness last night was fine as far as it went—but what about the ground ball that went through Leon Durham's legs in the fifth game of the playoffs against the San Diego Padres in 1984, which shattered the dreams of millions of Cubs fans from Chicago to *Eretz Yisrael*? As you can imagine, the more I thought about it, the more upset I got at this new rabbi's *chutzpah,* coming in like this, destroying tradition, practically outlawing the Cubs as an institution. Where in the *Torah* does it say "no Cubs on *Yom Kippur,*" huh, show me? Fortunately, I've calmed down a little now. . . .

So anyway, I've been thinking quite a bit about the messiah lately. To tell you the truth, I've always been a little jealous of the Christians, they having found their messiah and all. Well, at least he was one of our boys. Or so they say. Me, I'm not so sure he was—a Jewish carpenter? But anyway, Jewish or not, he had some pretty good qualities for a messiah—kind, good values. Frankly, though, I don't think he was the real messiah.

Why? Well nowhere do we read—not even in the *New Testament,* where the Christians could have stuck in pretty much anything they wanted—nowhere do we read that Jesus was much of an athlete. And I'm almost certain that the

messiah is going to turn out to be a pretty decent ballplayer.

By the way, for my fiftieth birthday last October, my wife surprised me and took me to Cooperstown to visit the

Baseball Hall of Fame. Did you know that in 1912 a Cubs player by the name of Henry "Heine" Zimmerman won the triple crown, batting .372, hitting 14 home runs and driving in 106 runs? It's true.

There isn't, strictly speaking, a Jewish section to the Hall of Fame, but I can pretty much tell you where they all are—the plaques of Sandy Koufax, who won the Cy Young Award in 1963, '65 and '66, and Hank Greenberg, who hit 56 home runs. The balls from Kenny Holtzman's no hitters. *Oy*, did I *kvell*.

But back to the messiah. Y'know there is an old *Hasidic* notion that the messiah may come in an unexpected form, and so one should treat everyone he encounters as if that person were the *mashiach*. I've been thinking about that and I'd like to be the first to announce that I'm pretty sure I've spotted him.

As you know, this has been a pretty dismal year for the Cubs pitching staff, with one exception. There's a 29-year old, 6'2" right hander from the Dominican Republic named José Bautista. In 1992, José pitched for Omaha in the American Association and Memphis in the double-A Southern League, compiling a brilliant record of two wins and ten losses, with a 4.90 ERA. Naturally, the Cubs scouts see this and they figure, "Oh boy, this is the type of guy who's going to fit in real well on our pitching staff." So they sign him. And what does José do this year? He's got a 9–3 record, with a 2.82 earned run average.

And, are you ready for this? José Bautista is Jewish. Honest. A conservative Jew. His son, Leo, goes to Hebrew school. They light *shabbos* candles . . . So, it's like the *Hasidim*

said, maybe you didn't expect the messiah to be a 6'2"
Dominican pitcher, but who knows?

And if José should turn out to be the messiah, there'll be
no problem on *Pesach*. I've tried it out, and I think José
Bautista will fit nicely into the song, instead of *Eliahu: José
Bautista-ha Navi*.[2] And, even if it doesn't fit, not to worry—
I've got Bob Applebaum[3] working on a new melody, a Latin
tune. Our cantor is going to have to learn to play the marim-
ba with her *klezmer* band.[4]

Now, of course, I know that one season does not necessarily
a *mashiach* make. But for a Jewish Cub fan, one good season by
a Jewish pitcher is not exactly chopped liver, either. And the
Hasids also say that we can't simply wait for the *mashiach*; we
must do our part to bring him. So watch José. And when he
comes in to pitch and doesn't give up any runs, do as I do—
say a *shehehianu*.

---

[2] Traditional Passover song.

[3] JRC congregant and composer of many melodies sung by the
congregation.

[4] JRC's cantor at the time, Lori Lippitz, directed a *klezmer* group
called *The Maxwell Street Klezmer Band*, which played traditional
Jewish music.

1994

Strike

The strike of 1994 was a blight on the history of baseball. There was no World Series; the season was in fact over two-thirds of the way through; and fans had little reason to expect the best. It might be said that all of baseball had a typical Chicago Cubs year.

As for the beleaguered Northsiders, the strike might have been a blessing in disguise. The Cubs fell 16½ games out of first place in the National League Central Division in just 113 games, going 49–64, so it was doubtful that 49 more contests would have helped. The season was all but sunk anyway when the Cubs set a 20th century National League mark by losing their first 12 games at Wrigley Field. Their first home victory didn't come until May 4, when they beat the Cincinnati Reds 5–2. Steve Trachsel picked up the victory. He finished the truncated season 9–7 with an ERA of 3.21, winding up fourth in the NL Rookie of the Year voting.

Bad got worse on June 13, when second baseman extraordinaire Ryne Sandberg announced his retirement, saying he had lost the desire to play a game that was "no longer fun." At the time of his retirement, Sandberg was fourth on the team's all-time list in home runs (245), sixth in hits and seventh in RBIs. He also had a .990 career fielding percentage, the highest ever for his position.

But, like Michael Jordan, who left basketball for a brief time to pursue a baseball career, Sandberg would suit up again for the Cubs in 1996. Cubs fans returned to their places even more quickly. They were among the first fans in baseball to reach their old attendance numbers when the strike ended in 1995.

. . . .

The Bright Side of the Strike

ARE YOU THE SAME GROUP? I mean were all of you here last year? I hate to have to start all over again, with the same *mishigas* every year. Look, if you weren't here, you'll just have to ask somebody who was, okay?

I mean, I'm here every year. So why shouldn't you be? I put a hell of a lot of work into these talks. It's not something I just whip up after *Kol Nidre*, you know.

For example, on the second day of *Rosh Hashanah* last year I have to rush straight from services to Wrigley Field. This is not a pleasure trip; I'm on assignment. I have to figure out whether José Bautista, the Cubs Jewish pitcher from the Dominican Republic, is the messiah. So I called the Cubs office and told them I needed a press pass to get onto the field to talk to Bautista. It's true, here's my pass, and here's the autographed picture I got from José.

So I get down onto the field—Wrigley Field—the same field that Ernie Banks, Billy Williams, Phil Cavaretta, Hank

Sauer, Frankie Baumholtz, Harry Chiti[1] played on. Now, I don't know whether, technically, we Reconstructionist Jews believe in heaven, but I certainly do. I was there. There I am, mingling down on beautiful Wrigley Field among Mark Grace and Ryne Sandberg—not talking to them, mind you, I was much too excited for that, just mingling.

I spot Steve Stone; you know Steve Stone, the former Cy Young award-winning pitcher who is now the Cubs' announcer, the guy who corrects Harry Caray when he says "we're in the bottom of the 6th, fans, and the Cubs trail the Montreal Expos 4–3," when it's really the top of the eighth and the Cubs are ahead of the Florida Marlins, 7–2. Anyway, I see Steve Stone and I know that Stone is Jewish, and, remember, this is the second day of *Rosh Hashanah.* So I screw up my courage and I go over to Stone (who is smoking a disgusting cigar) and I stick out my hand and say, *"Shana Tova."* Steve looks at me kinda funny, then sticks his hand out and says, "Steve Stone." I am not making this up.

I know that at least some people listen to my open mike talks. Because this year Boris Furman, JRC's irrepressible social committee chairman, organized the first annual José Bautista Day at Wrigley Field. I'll admit, I wasn't sure how many people we'd get, just putting a small notice in the JRC newsletter. But I've got to hand it to Boris, there were over 34,000 people out there that day. We should sell advertising in the newsletter, and cut our membership dues in half.

---

[1] All former Cubs stars, except Chiti who was a mediocre catcher—and that's a generous assessment.

Anyway, José Bautista Day was a beautiful, sunny day. And the Cubs won, 3-0. And José didn't even have to pitch. God works in mysterious ways. By the way, I think the jury's still out as to whether José is the messiah. It's true his earned run average went way up this year. But, hey, even the messiah is entitled to an off year.

Of course, what weighs heavily on all of our minds this *Yom Kippur* is the baseball strike. I have searched my soul to see whether, perhaps, there was something I did to bring this upon us. Should I have been kinder to my children? Walked my dog, Rubovits, a few more times? But I concluded, no, I've been pretty-much perfect again this year. Why, then, I asked myself, why do we have this strike?

So, I did what I usually do when I am confronted by these kinds of existential questions, I turned to the *Torah*, which is actually a very good scroll, if you haven't read it lately. By the way, it's a good thing that they decided to put the *Torah* into book form. If you think it's hard to read the *Tribune* sports section on the El,[2] just imagine trying to scroll your way through *Leviticus* while the train lurches along.

But I digress. Anyway, turning to the *Torah*, I was reminded of all of the apparently horrible things that happened to the Jewish people that actually turned out to be really fortunate. I can't think of any examples of those things, off hand, but there are plenty of them in there, I'm sure.

Could it be, I wondered, that the baseball strike was actually

---

[2] El is short for "elevated," the public transportation that stops half a block from Wrigley Field.

good for the Jews or, what to me is the same thing, good for Cubs fans? So I looked back at last season's standings and I saw that the Cubs lost 78 games last year. This year, however, thanks to the strike, they lost only 64 games. That is the fewest games the Cubs have lost in a season since 1945. And, remember, this October will be the first time since 1945— forty-nine years—that Cubs fans will not have to watch two other teams play in the World Series. So let us give thanks as we say, *"baruch atah adonai eloheynu melech haolam,* who creates the baseball strike when enough is enough, already."

1995

Bouncing Back

If Rip Van Winkle had waited until September of 1975 to embark on his fabled nap, he would have awoken 20 years later to see that the 1995 Cubs finished 73–71, four games behind Colorado for the National League Wild Card spot.

Colorado? Wild Card? Cubs above .500? And didn't they used to play more games than this? Baseball underwent massive structural change and expansion in the 80s and 90s, but the progress the Cubs made in the year after the strike of '94 wasn't too shabby, either. Calling the pitiful '94 season on account of greed had been like euthanasia to the struggling Cubs. But shortening the '95 season by almost four weeks as the players' strike finally ended (explaining those 19 missing games) may have cost the Cubs a shot at their first post-season appearance of the decade. The club never fell out of the top few spots in their division and held first place for all but one day before June 4. They finally settled on third, their best finish since winning the division in '89.

Not bad for a team that sank quicker than a Greg Maddux fork-ball the previous season. The 24-victory improvement bumped them from the third-worst record in the majors to the sixth-best record in the National League—only four teams made a more dramatic turnaround. New manager Jim Riggleman surely had something to do with that, as did some shrewd early-season acquisitions, including 14-game winning right-hander Jaime Navarro and well-rounded outfielder Brian McRae. First baseman Mark Grace ranked fifth in the league with a .326 batting average and fell six doubles shy of tying the club record of 57 two-baggers in a season. Outfielder Sammy Sosa's rare combination of power and speed produced 36 home runs and 34 stolen bases. Sosa's second 30/30 year made him one of just six major-leaguers ever to achieve that feat twice in a career.

The franchise reached two milestones in '95. The Cubs became the first single-city major league franchise to win 9,000 games when Sosa launched a solo home run in the 13th inning to beat the Los Angeles Dodgers 2–1 on May 21. Twelve weeks later, also against the Dodgers, Sosa rapped the Cubs' 10,000th home run. Even sluggers as accomplished as Sosa don't often get to hit a 10-grand slam.

● ●

Forgiving Grudgingly

THIS HAS BEEN A YEAR of deep spiritual crisis for me. So I called the rabbi recently, to request a meeting.

"Is it urgent?" he asked.

"Sort of," I replied.

"May I ask what it concerns?"

"Well I suppose if you're going to help me, you'll have to know what it concerns."

"I mean, may I ask over the phone?" he explained.

"Yes. It's baseball, the Cubs."

"*Oy vey,* then you'd better rush right over. How long do you think we'll need?"

"About four weeks," I estimated.

"Well, let me see, I have five *bar mitzvahs* scheduled, four weddings, three *brisses,* two funerals and a partridge in a pear tree. But I'll cancel them."

So I hied myself over to the *shul.* After we exchanged *shaloms,* the rabbi got straight to the point. "So, *nu?*" he asked.

"I've lost my faith," I said.

"I see that, it looks like you are becoming a Hare Krishna."

"No, I'm not becoming a Hare Krishna. I just happen to be getting bald, and you said to rush right over, so I didn't change out of my bathrobe and thongs."

"I see, then tell me, what seems to have caused this loss of faith?"

"The strike."

"The strike?"

"Yes, the baseball strike. I have lost interest in baseball."

"Lost interest? But what about Cal Ripken[1]?"

"*Ripken, Shmipken.* So he shows up every day for fourteen years. Big deal. If he'd been injured a couple days—or if his manager had made him take a day or two off, like he should

---

[1] Baltimore third baseman Cal Ripken broke Lou Gehrig's record for consecutive games played.

have—nobody would know his name. Besides, we Jews have had much longer streaks."

"What're you talking about?"

"Moses, in the desert, shows up forty years in a row—14,600 consecutive days. And he didn't have an off season."

"But you've been such an avid Cubs fan . . ."

"I've lost interest in the Cubs, too. Usually, I go to twenty games a season. This year I went to two."

"But the Cubs were right in the thick of the wild card race. How could you have lost interest?"

"Oh, it's all a business, there's no sport anymore."

"But baseball's been a business for a long time. Surely you knew that before the strike."

"Yes, I knew it. We all knew it. But we pretended different. The strike destroyed all of our illusions."

"You sound very hurt, and angry."

"I am. That's why I came to you for advice."

"Well, you know what is coming up soon, don't you?"

"Of course I do, the World Series."

"No, I meant the High Holidays."

"Oh, yes, I forgot."

"And what are we Jews supposed to do for the Holidays?"

"Repent."

"Very good, that's right, and what else?"

"Unuh . . . oh no, I'm not forgiving. Besides, the offender is supposed to ask forgiveness, and the Cubs haven't asked me."

"Sure they did. Didn't they sell their tickets at half price through May?"

"A cheap trick to try to draw people in when the weather was lousy."

"You are being too harsh. Remember, God forgave the Israelites for building the Golden Calf, so can't you forgive the baseball owners and players for trying to slay the Golden Goose?"

So I have thought about what the rabbi said. And maybe I should forgive them; I don't know, I just don't know.

By the way, for those of you who may still be wondering, José Bautista is definitely not the messiah. He pitched for the San Francisco Giants this year, his earned run average soared to 6.44, and his record dropped to 3–8. Of course, in the off season, the Cubs will probably trade Mark Grace and Shawon Dunston to the Giants to get old José back.[2]

But, hey, how about that *Sammela* Sosa? I think maybe that big gold chain he wears around his neck has a *chai* on it.

Oh, what the heck; Rabbi, you're right . . . I forgive.

*La shana ha ba-a b'*Wrigley Field.

---

[2] The Cubs have a history of bad trades, perhaps the worst of which was trading budding superstar, Lou Brock, to the St Louis Cardinals for a pitcher who never amounted to anything, Ernie Broglio.

1996

A Bad Break

The Cubs lost in 1996 because of bad pitching. Their pitchers set a variety of records, from the positive, most strikeouts in a season (1,027), to the opposite, most home runs allowed (184).

But, the Cubs' hopes for the year were dashed by a single pitch, from Florida's Mark Hutton, that severely fractured Sammy Sosa's hand on August 20. Catcher Scott Servais was hit by 14 pitches, a club record, but it was the fastball to Sosa that sunk the Cubs' season. Sosa had already belted 40 homers and driven in 100 RBIs by that time, and, with his 18 stolen bases, was on pace to become the first player since Willie Mays in 1955 to hit 50 home runs and steal 20 bases in a season. He sat out with the busted paw until 1997, and the Cubs went from a scant $3\frac{1}{2}$ games out of first place on August 21 to 12 games out by the season's end, losing 14 of their last 16 games and finishing fourth in the Central Division with a record of 76–86.

Despite his early exit, Sosa was third among National League outfielders with 15 assists, just one part of a defensively sound team. The Cubs committed a National League-low 104 errors en

route to a club-record .983 fielding percentage. Ryne Sandberg's
return at age 36 after almost two years in retirement only bolstered
those numbers. He ranked second among second basemen in field-
ing percentage, committed no throwing errors and broke Rogers
Hornsby's NL mark for career home runs at that position with his
265th. First baseman Mark Grace added a fourth Gold Glove to his
trophy case and batted .331 for the year.

Clearly, the Cubs had talent. But by losing 34 one-run games
and blowing a league-high 34 saves, the Cubs could only watch
helplessly as the man they let get away, Greg Maddux, helped the
Atlanta Braves win the World Series.

* *

Why Reconstructionists are Cubs Fans

AM OFTEN ASKED two questions. "Mr. Kanter, exactly what
is the derivation of the modern *kippah?*" and "Why are all
Reconstructionist Jews Cubs fans?" Well, as it happens, the
two are closely related.

First, as to the derivation of the modern *kippah.* It is true
that the *kippah,* when you examine it closely, is an odd
garment. I mean, other than for a hair-challenged guy like
me, what protection does it provide? Not much. So, are we
to conclude that it had no useful purpose, ever? Not on your
life, *bubbelah.* Listen up.

I have been studying the writings of the famous Jewish
archeologist, Bernie Ha Levi. Bernie is accredited by most
historians with the discovery of the Third Temple.
Interviewed by *Time* magazine after his incredible discovery,

Bernie, in typical, self-effacing manner, said, "Hey, I figured they built one temple; somebody knocked it down. They built a second one; somebody knocked it down. So why would they stop at two?" It is Bernie who, in describing the dispersal of the Jews after the destruction of the Third Temple, coined the word "Triaspora."[1] But I digress.

Anyway, let me quote directly from page 398 of Bernie's archeological classic, *Holy Holes:*

"So I was digging and digging, and, whew, was it hot. I'm telling you, you think you know hot, you don't know hot, this was hot. So I come across something that looked like a *kippah,* except it had a long bill on it. And I say to myself, 'Hey, Bernie, wonder what this thing is?' I talk to myself a lot. Out loud. But that's neither here nor there. Well, actually, it was there.

"So, anyway, I start to put this thing on my head, until my wife, Ethel, who had packed a gorgeous picnic lunch for the dig—corned beef (extra lean), kosher pickles, a thermos of lattes, the whole schmear—said, 'Bernie, what are you, nuts, putting that on your head? That thing's filthy dirty. It's been buried in the ground maybe two, three thousand years.'"

"But it looks like a *kippah,*" I said, "and it's got this bill on it."

"So? That means you've got to put that *schmutzig* thing on your head?"

So, I took the thing and smacked it against my hip a couple of times to sterilize it, and I began to inspect it more carefully,

---

[1] The Jews dispersal after the destruction of the second temple is referred to as the Diaspora.

and to speculate what it might have been used for. Then, suddenly, I shouted to Ethel, "Hey, Ethel, it is a *kippah*."

"How do you know that, Einstein?" Ethel asked.

"Because, look here, inside this one it says, in gold, 'Jesus' Bar Mitzvah, December 25, 13 C.E.' And, here's one that says, 'Maccabee Brothers Funeral Home' and this one says, 'Abraham and Sarah's Wedding.'"

"But, if that's a *kippah*, why did they put a bill on it?" Ethel asked.

"Well, in the days of yore," I explained, "it was open air; they had no roof in the old temples. So during services, they probably needed something to keep the sun out of their eyes. Look, see, this one has sun glasses attached to the inside of the bill so you can flip them down."

Ethel inspected the front of the *kippah* closely and said to me, "Okay, genius, explain this to me. What's the big red C on the front for?"

Well I was temporarily stumped. I thought and I thought. Cardinals? No. Cleveland? No. Cubs? . . . No. Finally I figured it out and I said to Ethel, "Ethel, the C probably stands for Chosen. You know, we were the Chosen People."

"But why did they need a C on it? Everybody at the old temples was chosen."

"Sure, but the idol worshippers worshipped outside, also, and they had hats, too. So the Jews needed the C to distinguish them."

Anyway, further research by Bernie showed that once *shuls* were built with roofs on them, the bills had outlived their usefulness. So bills were cut off of *kippot* as a cost-saving measure. The *C* was dropped because, once services were moved indoors, all other religions had the good sense to drop *kippot* altogether (except the Pope, of course, who apparently didn't get the message), so there was no need to distinguish any more. And, so, that's the derivation of the modern *kippah.*

But why, then, you ask, are all Reconstructionist Jews Cubs fans? That's really quite simple. As you know, Mordecai Kaplan, our founder, in his great wisdom, decided to ditch the notion of chosenness altogether in our liturgy. But, deep down, we all want to feel chosen, even Reconstructionists. And so it is because of this deep, primeval connection we Reconstructionist Jews feel to the old Chosen *kippot* that we all are Cubs fans.

So, the next time you're out at Wrigley Field, and Harry[2] leads the singing in the seventh inning, remember, the correct words, "For it's root, root, root for the *Cho–sen*, if they don't win it's a *shanda* . . . "

*La Shana, ha ba-a b'*Wrigley Field.

---

[2] Cubs announcer, Harry Caray, who started the tradition of singing "Take Me Out to the Ball Game" as the fans stretched in the seventh inning.

1997

Retiring Fourteens

In the game-by-game record of the 1997 Cubs, the first 14 dates each have a capital L next to them. After the New York Mets mercifully lost to the Cubs on April 20 to end the streak, first baseman Mark Grace declared, "Thank God. We won a game. We're 1–14. That's atrocious, but I'm going to have a little fun tonight." Grace's candid, upbeat reaction no doubt stems from the fact that he had been a Cub his entire major league career.

That 14-game skid set the National League record for most consecutive losses to begin a season, and helped assure that the 1997 Cubs would not crawl above fourth place in their five-team division. They didn't win their lucky seventh game until May 2, by which time they had 22 losses, and settled into fifth place on June 8. When the St. Louis Cardinals beat them in the last game of the season, it was loss number 94, the most capital L's for the Cubs since 1980.

This season was probably not the farewell tour that Ryne Sandberg imagined when the legendary second-baseman announced his re-retirement on August 2, effective at the end of the year. He had been a Cub since 1981, for 2,151 games. In that stretch, he set

major-league records for home runs (277) and fielding percentage
(.989) at second base. Only one Cub had more stolen bases, three
had more hits and five had more RBIs. Sandberg was a 10-time
All-Star, a 9-time Gold Glove recipient and a likable guy, to boot.

After he won his MVP award in 1984, Sandberg's high school
retired his number. No one who plays for North Central High
School in Spokane, Washington will again wear number 14 on his
uniform, just as no Cub player will ever again wear Mr. Cub's,
Ernie Banks, number 14. And Cubs fans hoped to retire another 14;
the 14-loss experience of 1997.

● ●

Kashering the Cubs

FIRST OFF, I WANT TO SAY that I don't think the Cubs had
nearly as bad a season as most people think they did.

The Bulls win 69 games and everyone is ecstatic.
Well—big deal and whoop-de-do—the Cubs won 68 games.
You say but the Cubs lost 83 more games than the Bulls. And
I say, why do you always have to dwell on the dark side of
everything? So it took the Cubs a few more games. Are you
in such a big hurry? You're on your way to a fire or something? But, then, we Jews are used to this double standard,
aren't we, so we shouldn't be so surprised when it's applied
to our baseball team.

But, if you still think they had a bad year, consider this: in
the first fourteen games this season, the Cubs were 14 games
under .500. In the next 148 games, though, they fell only
another 12 games under .500. Talk about improvement. If

they continue to improve at this rate, next season . . . should be a lot like this season.

Okay, so it wasn't such a great season. The question is why? I have a theory. Now I know that we Jews have a tendency to lapse into blaming ourselves for everything, into a kind of self-loathing. And I certainly don't want to fall into that trap. But my theory is that the Cubs are losing because we Reconstructionist Jewish Cubs fans are not taking the game seriously enough, not doing our part. To put it bluntly, instead of integrating our Judaism into baseball, we have forsaken baseball for *Torah*.

Let me give you a couple examples of how far we've fallen. How many of you remember the legendary Jewish pitcher, Sandy Koufax? Great. Now, tell me, how many of you can tell me the name of the Torah portion at Sandy Koufax's *bar mitzvah* and who catered the luncheon, afterwards? Uh-huh, I thought so. Okay, here's another one. How many of you can tell me the year that the Cubs last played in the World Series? No, not 1945; everyone knows that. The *Jewish* year.

But, you say to me, what about the Baltimore Orioles? They won their division this year. Did they have Jewish support? And why blame the Reconstructionists? What are the Orthodox doing? Well, I'm glad you asked.

I read to you now from the *Washington Post* on May 6, 1996 sent into me by an alert reader. And, as Dave Barry[1] would say, I am not making this up.

---

[1] Prolific and very funny humorist. I don't know whether he's Jewish.

It was the bottom of the fifth, two out, and the Orioles batter popped out to the catcher, ending a brief rally. As the O's took the field, a bit despondently, Saul Newman headed for a prayer session.

It had nothing to do with the fact that the Orioles were trailing badly and needed help, heavenly and earthly, in a game that was going south on them. Newman is an Orthodox Jew who prays three times a day, as custom prescribes, and he was heading off to join other Jews for their afternoon prayers in a small room behind the kosher food stand at Section 32 of Camden Yards.

The article also said, "a rabbi from Greenbelt wore an orange Orioles cap during the afternoon prayers, known as *mincha*." I'll bet the rabbi didn't even have a hat like mine that has the Cubs team name in Hebrew.[2]

But I digress. So, in Baltimore, they have a kosher food stand (potato *knishes* go for a buck seventy-five) and Jews praying, and the Orioles are winning big. It doesn't seem like much of a mystery to me as to what the Cubs need. And I'm going to fire off a letter to Cubs management to see if I can get the ball rolling. I have a couple ideas. For one thing, it occurs to me that, by now, maybe the Cubs old shortstop, Ivan de Jesus, has a kid who's ready to play major league ball. Wouldn't you just love to be a member of the Jews for de Jesus fan club? And another thing I think I'll suggest is that the Cub organization might help things along a little by hiring a general manager whose last name was not MacPhail.[3] How about the ex-pitcher, Early Wynn?[4]

Anyway, with these changes (and, of course, the kosher food and Mogen David wine vendors, and the new davening area in the center field bleachers), there's only one more thing we need to do—find a way to get to Harry Caray. Maybe we could do it through Steve Stone, who is an *MOT*.[5] Although, come to think of it, that may not be so promising. Most of you probably remember how in 1993, on my way

---

[2] See the hat in the picture of the author on the back cover.
[3] Larry MacPhail, General Manager of the Cubs.
[4] Former Cleveland Indians and Chicago White Sox pitching great.
[5] Member of the Tribe, sometimes used to mean Jewish.

off the field from interviewing José Bautista between *Rosh Hashanah* and *Yom Kippur,* I saw Steve Stone. I stuck my hand out and said, *"Shana Tova."* And, he paused a second, then put his hand out and said "Steve Stone." So maybe Steve's not our man.

But, why do we need to get to Harry, anyway, you ask? I would have thought that would be obvious to you—to convince Harry that in the seventh inning we ought to be singing, "For it's *echad, shtayim, shalosh* strikes you're out at the old ball game."[6]

*La shana, ha ba-a b'*Wrigley Field.

---

[6] Sadly, after 16 years as the Cubs announcer, Harry Caray died during the off season. A statue of him with his microphone, leading "Take Me Out to the Ball Game," now stands outside Wrigley Field.

1998

Caraying Out a Plan

In 1908, the last season the Cubs won the World Series, the entire team hit 19 home runs. And, thirty years later, in 1938, they managed just 65. Sixty years after that, though, in 1998, Sammy Sosa alone belted 66 home runs.

Thus, the baton of Chicago's favorite athlete passed smoothly in June—from Michael Jordan, who won a sixth world championship in his final game as a Chicago Bull, to Sammy Sosa, who hit a major-league record 20 home runs that same month. Sosa's home run tug-of-war with St. Louis Cardinal slugger Mark McGwire captured the imagination of the nation. McGwire, who was first to break Roger Maris' 37-year-old record of 61 home runs, didn't quit until he hit 70. Sosa wound up with the second-highest total ever, 66, and added 158 runs batted in, for good measure.

Even more remarkable than the gaudy home run totals, though, the Cubs were actually winning. And not just on account of Sosa's hot bat. In only his fifth major league start, National League Rookie of the Year Kerry Wood tied a major-league record by striking out 20 Houston Astros, a performance that Sports Illustrated *labeled the most dominant pitching performance ever. Reliever Rod Beck tested*

Cubs fans' hearts all season, as he collected a club-record 51 saves.

It took a one-game playoff victory over the San Francisco Giants for the Cubs to earn a trip to the playoffs (for the first time in nine years); but there they were, in the postseason, as a Wild Card Team (what more fitting appellation for the Cubs than that?), battling the Atlanta Braves. Not surprisingly, the Braves swept the three games, restoring the Cubs to their rightful place in the order of the universe.

But the endearingly humble Sosa was the overwhelming choice as National League MVP. And the Cubs proved just as lovable as winners as they've always been as losers.

●●

Glimpsing the Promised Land

I WOULD LIKE TO SPEAK TODAY about maturity.

I am not a mature person. While my wife and daughters would point to hundreds of examples to prove this beyond any reasonable doubt, I prefer not to wallow in those reasons today. Instead, I would like to focus on just one—the Chicago Cubs.

To give me my due, I've made progress. Not long ago, my moods could swing dramatically with a Bulls or a Bears win or loss. Now, frankly, I couldn't care less whether the Bulls play this year. And about the only thing I'd sorta like to see in the remainder of the pro football season is Mike Ditka[1] lose all the rest of his games.

---

[1] Former head coach of the Chicago Bears, now coach of the New Orleans Saints. A brash, controversial figure—and not my favorite person.

It's just the Cubs I care about now. I'll grant you that I may take this to extremes. About a month ago, for example, we got a new puppy to go with our main dog, Rubovits. My wife, Carol, and I disagreed over what to name the puppy. Ultimately, I prevailed by making Carol a deal—if Sammy hit a home run that day, we'd name the puppy Sosa. Not that the other name we were considering, Wrigley, would have been so bad either.

But, I do not spend my time watching Cubs games frivolously. For me, it is an intensely Jewish experience. For starters, I always wear my Hebrew Cubs hat. Let me give you a few more examples of what I mean by a Jewish experience.

On June 5, in the seventh inning of the Cubs–White Sox game, I found myself pondering why the blessing over the wine did not read simply, *"Baruch atah adonai, eloheinu melech haolam, shenatan lanu yayin."* "Blessed are you, God, who has given us wine." Not atypically, the Cubs had blown a 5–2 lead. With the game tied and a runner on first, the Sox batter hit a shot to right center, and, as the runner on first rounded third with what would have been the winning run, the ball stuck in the ivy. The Sox runner was sent back to third and the Cubs won the game in the 12th inning, with a home run. An epiphany struck me: the blessing over the wine, *boray p'ree hagafen*—who has given us the fruit of the vine—was originally (and, properly understood, is still today), a baseball blessing for Cubs games at Wrigley Field.

Another significant game for me was the August 24 game against the Houston Astros. Some of you may recall the driving rain that day, a flood of Biblical proportions, that delayed the game almost two hours. A couple weeks before that game, anticipating a spiritual crisis on the 24th, I had called our new rabbi to ask if he would counsel me at Wrigley Field. Selflessly, he accepted.

While, of course, I can't tell you everything that Rabbi Rosen and I discussed, much of which was incredibly personal—and I'd be the last to reveal all that he confided in me—I can tell you that a portion of our time was spent discussing the arcane, but extremely important, question—much debated in the Talmud—of how one converts from being a Colorado Rockies fan to a Cubs fan.[2] The answer is that it takes three things: intense study of former Cubs greats, especially Jewish players like Ken Holtzman[3] (fortunately for the rabbi, it's a short list); attending a *bat din*[4] (which is the noise created by a lot of Cubs hits); and a trip to the *mikva* at the Cubby Bear.[5] I am working assiduously with the rabbi, and hope to have his conversion completed by opening day, 1999.

Then, on September 13th, Carol, Jodi and I saw Sammy Sosa's 61st and 62nd home runs, against the Brewers. Though that wasn't, as they say in baseball, chopped liver, even better was the Cubs rally from way back to tie the game in the 9th and then win it in the 10th on a home run by Mark

---

[2] Rabbi Brant Rosen, an avid baseball fan, moved to JRC from Denver, where he was a partial season ticket holder of the Colorado Rockies.

[3] Former Cubs pitching star who threw two no-hitters.

[4] A *beit din* is a panel of rabbis who, among other things, validate a conversion.

[5] A watering hole for Cubs fans, near Wrigley Field.

Grace—get this—on Gracie the Swan Beanie Baby Day. Is that the definition of *bashert,* or what?

Jewish experiences are not all so rosy, though. On September 23, I watched the entire Cubs-Brewers game on TV. Had you been in my house that afternoon, you would have thought that at least one person had died when you heard me screaming at the TV, "NO! NO! NO!" as Brant Brown[6]

---

[6] A young Cubs outfielder. The fly ball he dropped cost the Cubs the game, and almost cost the team the Wild Card position.

dropped the last out, allowing three runs to score. Of course, silent between my "NO! NO! NO!" were the words "NOT AGAIN! NOT AGAIN! NOT AGAIN!" Immediately, in my misery, I pulled out and reread the *Book of Job.*

Finally, two nights ago at Wrigley Field, in the playoff game for the wild card spot, I glimpsed the Promised Land, as the Cubs beat the Giants 5–3. I may never get there but, hey, neither did Moses.

To further show the progress I'm making toward maturity, today, on *Yom Kippur,* I'd like to forgive two people publicly. First, Brant Brown for dropping that fly ball. How can I continue to harbor a grudge against a ball player who is about the same age as my two daughters? And besides, it was Brant Brown who hit the winning home run in the 12th inning against the White Sox in the *boray p'ree hagafen* game on June 5. And second, I'd like to forgive our rabbi for having the same first name as Brant Brown.

But in another sense, as I admitted earlier, I am not a mature person. I still care deeply about the Cubs. I still love few things better than being out at Wrigley Field. I think maturity is grossly overrated, anyway. I'm hoping never to reach it completely—and I think I've got a damn good shot at achieving that goal.

There have been times when I've wondered whether talking about the Cubs on *Yom Kippur* was an irreligious thing to do. It's not. Can you image a more spiritual experience than walking into Wrigley Field on a sunny afternoon, seeing the green of the grass and the ivy on the walls, and sitting among a true community of 38,000 people who exude nothing but love towards a multiracial group of men who they are pretty darn sure are ultimately going to lose?

In closing, I'd like to repeat what Sammy Sosa said, in another language, *"Kadur basis tov meod, tov meod aylai."*[7]

*L'Shana Ha ba-a b'*Wrigley Field.

---

[7] "Baseball's been very, very good to me."

1999

End of a Millennium (at last)

On June 8, the Cubs seemed poised to repeat their 1998 success. Nine games above .500, just a game and a half out of first place in the National League Central, the veteran Cubbies looked loaded and ready for another playoff run.

For some teams, though, that shoe doesn't fit. For the Cubs, it was their Sox that gave them fits.

After taking two of three from the hot Arizona Diamondbacks in Phoenix, the Cubs returned to Wrigley Field to host their cross-town rivals, the Chicago White Sox. The Cubs dropped three straight to the Sox. Then they dropped off the face of the planet by losing 59 of their next 84 games.

Included in that Chernobylesque melt-down was an all-time franchise low 6–24 record in August and an equally ignominious 2–10 out of the blocks in September. The team that was flirting with .600 shortly after Memorial Day needed their own memorial service by Labor Day.

The season may have been doomed when 1998 Rookie of the Year Kerry Wood was lost for the year—and potentially his

career—with an elbow injury. Closer Rod Beck, another 1998 hero,
was out for most of the season with bone spurs in his elbow, then
was traded to the Red Sox.

As usual, the season had its bright spots. Sammy Sosa became
the first major league player in history to hit 60 home runs in two
consecutive seasons, though Mark McGwire ultimately exceeded
Sammy's 1999 total of 63 home runs by two. Cubs first baseman
Mark Grace garnered a total of 1754 hits in the 90s, more hits than
any other player in the decade. Finishing second to Grace was
an outfielder the Cubs traded away to the Texas Rangers, Rafael
Palmeiro, thus reminding Cubs fans one last time of the century
that might have been.

Is God a Cubs Fan?

AS WE MEET, the Cubs are 60–89, 31 games out of first, and possessors of the third worst record in all of baseball. A season like the one we're suffering through tests a Cub fan's faith—and stupidity. I score high in both tests.

The season also causes thoughtful folks (like me, for instance) to raise important, serious questions; questions that may challenge assumptions we've made all our lives; assumptions so strong we may not even have been aware we've made them. I'd like to discuss one such assumption today by asking, "Is God a Cubs fan?"

But before I do, I'd like to put to rest another question that

we left hanging last *Yom Kippur,* a question that may have
been troubling many of you (consciously or not) throughout
this season. You'll recall that shortly before the 1998 High
Holidays, Rabbi Brant Rosen arrived on our doorstep from
Denver, an open and notorious partial-season ticket holder of
the Colorado Rockies. Immediately, I began his conversion.
Brant took well to his exposure to Wrigley Field in late 1998
and studied intensely to become a Cubs fan in the off season.

Before the 1999 season, Brant called me and reported that
he had become a Cubs fan. Now I don't want you to think
that I don't trust our rabbi, but I was trained as a lawyer and
I don't trust anybody. So I conceived of a simple plan to test
him. On May 4, I invited Brant out to a Cubs-Rockies game.
During the game, I scrutinized his every move. He *kvelled*
when the Cubs scored 4 runs in the third, 3 in the fourth and
1 in the fifth to take an 8–2 lead. He grimaced when the
Rockies retaliated with 3 in each of the sixth, seventh and
eighth to go ahead 11–8. He was on his feet when the Cubs
tied it 11–11 in the bottom of the eighth. He consoled me
when the Cubs gave up a run in the top of the ninth, and he
whooped (as best a rabbi can whoop) when the Cubs scored
two in the bottom of the ninth to pull it out, 13–12. So I can
report confidently that Brant's conversion is complete. Sorry
about that, Rabbi.

But it does not necessarily follow that because Brant is a
Cubs fan God must be, too. As a recovering lawyer, I can see
the fallacy in this reasoning. Indeed, we need to step back and
ask, preliminarily, whether God is a baseball fan at all. The

answer to that question is—of course God is a baseball fan. I
mean I'm willing to revisit fundamental assumptions, but let's
not get ridiculous here, okay? God not a baseball fan? Get real.

Now that we've established that God is a baseball fan, the
question remains—for whom does he root? Perhaps, you

may suggest, he does not root for any team. After all, he is the God of all baseball fans; our pain is his pain, so to speak. But remember that God sees all, which means he has season tickets for all 30 teams. (Pretty good seats, too. Between home and first, except in Wrigley Field. It seems that after the Cubs last pennant in 1945, God forgot to renew on time for the 1946 season, and they stuck him way down the right field line, beyond the visitors' bull pen.) But I digress . . . can you imagine how boring it would be for God to watch every baseball game and not have a team to root for?

But which team? Fortunately, we can eliminate certain teams confidently, right off the bat. For example, in Mordecai Kaplan's weighty tome, *Judaism as a Civilization*,[1] a little-noted passage that appears right after the section in which Kaplan debunks the notion that the Jews are God's chosen people says, "And the notion that God might be a Yankees fan must be repugnant to every modern Jew." I mean even Kaplan drew the line somewhere.

And certainly God would not root for a team in a domed stadium. Where's the connection to heaven there, I ask you? Nor could he be a fan of a new team, such as the Arizona Diamondbacks or the Tampa Bay Devil Rays. For whom would he have been rooting all those years before those teams came along? And God's not going to back a team that offends Native Americans; so, poof, there go the Braves with their tomahawk chant and the Cleveland Indians, the tribe.

---

[1] The central writing of the founder of Reconstructionism.

Unfortunately, I don't have time to run through all thirty teams, because the 3-minute time limit for Open Mike talks is being strictly enforced this year. So let me cut to the chase. Ultimately, it comes down to two teams. God could be either a Cubs fan or a Boston Red Sox fan. Indeed, sometimes those two teams seem indistinguishable. Both play in great old ball parks, neither has won a World Series in over 80 years, Cubs first baseman Leon Durham blew the 1984 pennant by letting a ground ball go through his legs and ex-Cubs first baseman Bill Buckner blew the World Series for the Red Sox with an error two years later.

How do we determine, then, whether God is a Cubs fan or a Red Sox fan? Simple: we do as the ancients did, we look for a sign. So all season long I sat out at Wrigley Field thinking, "Please God, give me a sign." I really concentrated on it, hard, "Please, God," I said to myself, "give me a sign. Are you a Cubs fan?" I watched everyone carefully for that sign—the coaches (who do give signs), the players, the fans, the umpires, the ushers, the beer vendors—everyone. When the seventh inning stretch came, I kept expecting the Cubs public address announcer, Paul Friedman, a Jew, to say, "Leading us in 'Take Me Out to the Ball Game' today will be the biggest Cubs fan of them all, *Ha Shem*."[2] And a deep, resonant voice would emanate from the booth, saying, "Okay, let me hear you, good and loud, *echad, shtayim, shalosh . . .*"

---

[2] In tribute to former Cub announcer Harry Caray, a celebrity guest now leads the singing of this song each game.

But none of that happened and I was beginning to despair. I thought I might have to wait until Sunday, September 26, for the last game in Wrigley Field this millennium—Millennium Beanie Baby Day for heaven's sake—for God's fandom to be revealed. I thought that until this Saturday, that is. (For those of you wondering why I was out at Wrigley Field on *shabbos*, let me remind you that it was a 3:05PM start and a Reconstructionist Cubs fan is permitted to go to any game on *shabbos* provided that *shabbos* will be over—that is, the ballpark lights will come on—before the end of the game.) So there I was in the sixth inning, when Sammy became the first player ever to hit 60 home runs in two seasons. And those of you who were there, or saw the replays on TV, you know what *Sammela* did as he rounded the bases. Yes, he pointed up at the sky, saluting the greatest Cubs fan of them all.

*L'millennium ha ba-a b'*Wrigley Field.

GLOSSARY

Akedah the Torah portion that includes the story of the binding of Isaac by Abraham

bar mitzvah ceremony in which 13-year old boy becomes an adult member of the Jewish community; the analogous female ceremony is the bat mitzvah

beit din a tribunal of rabbis convened as a Jewish court of law to decide cases brought before it, as, for example, to approve a conversion

bentched prayed

bashert meant to be

bimah raised platform, or stage

bochers guys, young men

bracha blessing

bris ritual circumcision

bubbelah term of endearment

chai life, in Hebrew; in the Hebrew numbering system, the letters *chayt* and *yod* (that spell the word *chai*) represent the number eighteen

challah braided bread traditionally eaten on Sabbath

Chanukah Jewish winter holiday known as the Festival of Lights

chazan(im) cantor(s)

chutzpah nerve, hubris

daven pray

echad, shtayim, shalosh one, two, three

Eretz Yisrael land of Israel

erev eve of a holiday, begins at sundown

frum meticulously observant

gefilte fish stewed or baked fish stuffed with a mixture of the fish flesh, bread crumbs, eggs, and seasoning, or prepared as balls or oval cakes boiled in a fish stock

goyim; goyish non-Jews; not Jewish

hasidic belonging to a sect of Jews that developed in 18th-century Poland and Russia

Ha Shem a name for God—literally, *The Name*

kippah (pl. *kippot*) skull cap(s) or yarmulke(s)

klezmer a type of traditional Jewish music

knish a small round or square of dough stuffed with a filling and baked or fried

Kol Nidre opening prayer of the evening service of *Yom Kippur*

kvell beam with pride

l'hadlik ner shel Cubbelas to light the Cubs' candle

*l'shanah ha ba-a b'***Wrigley Field** next year may we be in Wrigley Field

Leviticus the third book of the five books of Moses that make up the Torah

mashiach messiah

matzah unleavened bread eaten during Passover

mezzuzah (pl. *mezzuzot*) small container of scripture affixed to the door frames of Jewish homes

midrash (pl. *midrashim*) story that expands on or explains a portion of Torah *mikva* bath used in ritual purification and in conversion ceremonies

minhag(im) custom(s)

mishigas silliness or an oddity

mishuga crazy

nachas joy, pleasure

nosh snack

nu? so?

oy! oh!

oy vey! oh no! (literally, oh, woe!)

parsha a portion of the Torah

Pesach the holiday that celebrates the deliverance of the Jews from slavery in Egypt; also called Passover

Rosh Hashanah the beginning of the year on the Jewish calendar

schlep drag or carry

schmutzig dirty

shabbat shalom good Sabbath (literally a *Sabbath of peace*), a greeting on the Sabbath

shabbos Sabbath

shalom hello (also means good-bye and peace)

Shana Tova Happy New Year

shanda shame

shehehianu traditional prayer of thanksgiving

shomer shabbos observant of religious tenets for the Sabbath

shul synagogue

Torah the five books of Moses

trayf unkosher food

tzedakah charity as a religious obligation

vay iz meer! my gosh! (literally, woe is me!)

Yid a person who speaks Yiddish, a Jew

Yiddish language spoken by Jews of Europe

Yom Kippur the holiest day of the Jewish year, ten days after
Rosh Hashanah

yontiff holiday

BIOGRAPHIES
●●

ARNIE KANTER attends the JRC minyan and Cubs games. In between, he consults to major law firms and investment banks. Arnie has written a bunch of books, some serious and some humorous, but has difficulty determining which are which. His two daughters, Jodi and Wendy, have left the nest, so he lives in Evanston, Illinois, with his poet-psychotherapist wife, Carol, and their two way-above-average standard poodles, Rubovits and Sosa.

DARLENE GROSSMAN is the older of twin girls born on a day when the Cubs split a double header, losing the first game. She has a B.F.A. in graphic design and likes to color and play with type. Darlene freelances and works for a textbook publisher in Evanston when not at the JRC minyan. She and her husband, Ray, have three way-above-average standard children, Aryn, Maris, and Seth, and one adoring son-in-law, Ted.

SAM EIFLING studies journalism at Northwestern University and donates much of his free time to writing about sports for the *Daily Northwestern*. He touched Sammy's 61st home run ball in 1998, and plans to be in the press box the next time the Cubs go to the World Series, assuming he can still climb all those stairs at age 90.

ORDER FORM

To order additional copies of *Is God a Cubs Fan?*, please fill out the form below and send it with $14.95 plus $5.00 per order for shipping and handling, to:

IGCF, c/o JRC Press

303 Dodge Avenue

Evanston, IL 60202

Make checks or money orders payable to JRC.

Allow three weeks for delivery.

Number of copies: _____ x $14.95 each = $_____

Handling: $5.00

Total: $_____

Ship to:

Name: _____

Address: _____

_____

City: _____

State: _____ Zip Code:_____

Telephone: _____ / _____

E-Mail: _____